3-12-56
5-9-56

SEVEN STARS FOR CATFISH BEND

SEVEN STARS
FOR
CATFISH BEND

BY

BEN LUCIEN BURMAN

Illustrations by ALICE CADDY

FUNK & WAGNALLS COMPANY

NEW YORK

PUBLISHED BY FUNK & WAGNALLS COMPANY

153 EAST 24TH STREET, NEW YORK 10

© 1956 BY BEN LUCIEN BURMAN

ℓℓ

PRINTED IN THE UNITED STATES OF AMERICA

LIBRARY OF CONGRESS CATALOG CARD NUMBER 56-7770

1

ℓℓ

This book is for ANDREA herself

SEVEN STARS FOR CATFISH BEND

THE *Tennessee Belle* steamed down the Mississippi and blew a long whistle for Catfish Bend. We tied up at the bank so the engineer could fix some broken planks in the paddle wheel, and I thought I'd go on shore for a walk.

I was deep in the swamp back from the river when I heard a tree fall a little way off. I went on farther and I heard a funny sound, sort of like a food chopper, grinding something hard.

All of a sudden an animal burst out from the bushes. And then I saw it was my old friend, Doc Raccoon, of Catfish Bend.

"Jump!" he shouted.

I jumped in a hurry, just in time not to be hit by the tall pine tree beside me that came crashing down a few inches from my head.

A minute later a big old beaver came from the tree stump, his mouth full of wooden chips.

The raccoon turned to the beaver sternly. "You've got the wrong man," he said. "Watch where you're chopping."

The beaver mumbled an apology and shuffled away.

The raccoon came closer and we began to talk. I hadn't seen him for quite a while and I was shocked at the way he was looking. He was always a little shabby, but now his fur was caked with mud and all tangled with briars and burrs; here and there his skin showed gray where a patch of fur was missing. He was limping on one hind paw, too; I could see that he was all worn out.

"Looks like you've been having a rough time," I said.

"Rough?" he repeated. "Rough? If it'd been any worse I'd be dead. . . . Lend me a comb, will you? I'll feel better when I get my hair and whiskers straight."

I lent him what he asked for and he struggled with the tangles. Then he washed the comb in a pool of muddy water and offered it to me again.

"You better keep it," I said.

The coon polished it with his paw, and looking around to see that nobody was watching, hid it under a log. "It's been a terrible time. I didn't think any of us would come out alive. But we've won a wonderful victory. It's something the animals at Catfish'll be talking about for a thousand years."

And then he told me what happened.

The raccoon began:

I

I T started right here in this swamp. It was twilight, one of those pretty days you get at Catfish Bend in summer, and I was waiting for the old bullfrog to start rehearsing the other frogs in the Indian Bayou Glee Club for the concert they were giving next week down at Cypress Landing. You know the old bullfrog with the big folds of skin hanging down his face that make him look gloomy as a buzzard. I had to hold in my sides to keep from laughing, it was so funny the way his skin shook when he paced back and forth, humming and croaking, and telling the other frogs how to sing each part.

Well, all of a sudden some of the young frogs gave a wild jump, and I saw it was because Judge Black, the blacksnake, had come out of the bushes. They hadn't been around long enough to know that Judge Black, who'd been a judge over in Claiborne County, Mississippi, was a vegetarian and wouldn't bother 'em for anything.

And then a lot of wild ducks went

squawking off in a hurry and I saw J. C. the fox had come up to listen. You know J. C.—that's the way he likes us to call him. Kind of smart aleck and a terrible show-off, always talking and making a noise, and sometimes he'll almost scare some other animal to death, just for what he thinks is fun.

Well, the frogs were all ready to begin when the rabbit that always goes around with us had one of his giggling spells—he gets sillier and sillier all the time instead of smarter —and he giggled so hard the frogs couldn't start the rehearsal. And everybody was getting mad, and I told him to

think of a big head of lettuce. And he got so hungry the giggling stopped, and the Glee Club could go on with the singing.

The Club did fine, singing *Down, Deep Down In The Sea*, and things like that with low voices that are good for a frog.

They stopped for a while between numbers.

"Music has charms to soothe the savage breast," said Judge Black, the blacksnake, with one of the mottoes he was always using.

It got dark and a big moon came up over the bayou, and the frogs started singing again.

J. C. the fox, who like I said was always showing off, turned his head to the moon and began to howl in a terrible voice, thinking he was singing with 'em.

We shut him up in a hurry.

He looked hurt. "That was *Chop Sticks* I was singing," he said. "It goes fine with *Deep In The Sea*. Over back of West Memphis where I lived the frogs used to ask me to do it with 'em every time they sang."

I watched the moonlight coming down through the cypresses. "A night like this makes you realize how lucky we are to live at Catfish Bend," I said.

"I've been all around," croaked the frog. "I've sung in the swamps over as far as Mobile in Alabama and in Arkansas over to Little Rock, and in Tennessee as far as Chattanooga. Catfish Bend's the most wonderful place in the world."

And we all agreed.

None of us knew the terrible thing that was going to happen, before we were much older, that was going to change our whole lives.

Well, the frogs were starting a new song when all of a sudden there was a rifle shot.

"Run!" I shouted. "It's the hunter."

And we all scrambled into the bushes.

Everybody knows an ordinary man's bad enough, but a hunter's the worst kind of man anywhere. And this hunter was worse than the others. He hunted out of season when people weren't supposed to even shoot blanks just to scare you, when you were maybe borrowing a sweet potato or an ear of corn from a farm.

We hid behind the trees and we saw him coming down the bayou, steering a gas boat close along the shore. He was swinging a big searchlight trying to find us, and shooting a big gun if a blade of grass moved. He had a regular hunter's head, all tight and skinny, with wicked butcher eyes they say can hypnotize you if you don't turn away. And he had a hunter's nose, long and pointed like a pine needle, so he can smell you miles off in the wind—not like an animal's nose that's pretty and flat against your face.

I didn't have time to get to my own tree that had a fine hole to hide in, and so I had to take the first one I could find. It wasn't a good place and before I knew it, *ping!* a bullet whistled past me and then another and another, maybe six or seven shots, till the hunter had to stop and reload his gun.

I tell you it's bad enough having

somebody after you that's ten times as big as you are. But it's terrible when he's got a gun and you know he's trying to kill you, and all you can do is hide or run. And then that awful searchlight gets in your eyes so bad you're liable to do something crazy; it makes you as blind as a mole.

Well, by the time the hunter got his gun ready again, I jumped down and got away. He stayed around until daylight and didn't catch anybody. But I and plenty of other animals had a lot more white hairs in our fur.

When he was gone I came back to the bayou. And I saw that a squirrel-mother I knew had dropped one of her babies out of a tree when she was running with her family to hide from the hunter. The baby was laying on the ground, squeaking its head off, and I was just going up to help when I saw Judge Black, who was nearer than I was, pick it up in his mouth. And right away he started climbing the tree it fell from to put it back in the nest. He was half-way up when the mother and father squirrels, who had missed the baby

now, came running through the palmetto. The mother squirrel knew Judge
Black and knew how he was a vegetarian, and of course she wasn't worried.
But the father was a stranger, just come
to the Bend. When he saw the baby
squirrel in a snake's mouth, he began
carrying on like a wildcat, running up
the tree and screaming and clawing and
biting Judge Black's tail to make him let
go. And the mother squirrel was right
behind, screaming and telling him it was
all right, and trying to make him be
quiet.

The Judge didn't pay any attention
to the father's biting, though, and just
kept right on climbing. And he put the
baby back in the nest and then came
down again to the ground.

The mother thanked him and said she was sorry about her husband. He came from back in the hills and didn't know very much, she said, and didn't know what a fine snake the Judge was.

And Judge Black looked sad and said with a motto again, "The evil that men do lives after them." And he gave a sigh you could see going all the way along his body, from his mouth to his tail. "I've been spending all my life trying to live down the snakes' bad reputation. But sometimes, like today, I wonder if I ever can."

Well, things got quiet and we were thinking maybe we could get a little sleep, when there was another sound that made us scramble to the woods again, a funny barking and roaring, half-way between a dog and a bull. It was Old Joe, the alligator, on the prowl.

He came down the bayou, sloshing and splashing; with his awful jaws chewing and champing, he looked like one of those big steam shovels digging up sand from the Mississippi bottom.

I was up in another tree by now, too low to be really safe. He saw me and began swashing in circles around the trunk, trying to reach up and pull me down.

"Ararat," I called to him.

"What's that?" he hollered.

"Ararat," I told him again. "That's where Noah's Ark got stuck on a mountain. It's the code word when the animals signed the peace pact at Catfish Bend. Ararat means no more fighting."

"Ararat my hat," the alligator answered, and tried to climb the tree.

He went away after a while and I

could hear him rushing through the swamp. And then I heard a possum and a rabbit mother crying, and I saw a lot of possums and rabbits with their heads bowed going out to the animal cemetery. And I knew there wouldn't be any peace in the swamp until this hunting was ended.

So I called a meeting. "We've got to stop all this hunting," I said. "Hunting by alligators or hunting by men. Hunting's the worst thing anywhere."

Of course everybody agreed the way I knew they would.

We saw Old Joe just then going down the bayou, and we decided we'd start with him right away.

"A stitch in time saves nine," said Judge Black. "We'll have a trial."

"Have to catch him first," answered J. C. the fox. "And catching an alligator ain't eating watermelon."

Judge Black took one of the cough-drops he always used. "That's old-fashioned law," he said. "New fashion you try him first and catch him afterward. That way you know he's guilty and you don't catch any innocent people."

We started to get ready for the trial that day.

"With this kind of trial somebody has to act Old Joe," Judge Black said. "I've been trying to think who'd be best."

J. C. the fox spoke up fast. "I'll act him," he declared. "Whenever the animals around West Memphis gave a show I was always in it. And when I did my imitations they used to hold their sides laughing."

The judge said all right; and the day the trial started the fox put on an alligator skin we found on the bank, like he was Old Joe. And the frog was the lawyer against him, because he looked so gloomy and had such a deep voice besides. The judge made the rabbit be the lawyer for what they call the defense and say Old Joe was all right, though he didn't want to do it at all, because of the way alligators treat rabbits. But the law's the law, Judge Black said, and you have to be fair to everybody, even alligators.

Well, the animals came from miles around to say how terrible Old Joe was, foxes and raccoons and rabbits and squirrels, and even pigs and dogs from the farm at the edge of the swamp to tell how he'd eaten their little pigs and puppies. All the time the fox in the alligator skin pretending to be Old Joe kept running back and forth, whipping his tail and rolling his eyes, and shouting it wasn't so.

"I'm a good alligator," he hollered. "You won't believe a pig, will you?

Everybody knows there's nothing more slippery than a pig. When you talk against somebody you don't say he acts like an alligator. You say he acts like a pig." He whipped his tail over the ground again till it stirred up dust like a whirlwind. "And that big collie and the shepherd dog on the farm. You can't believe them either. They're mad because I saw 'em sneaking off to town last week when they were supposed to be watching their sheep. They're afraid I'll tell the farmer."

And the pig and the dogs kind of turned white.

I tell you that fox had a brain all right. I almost believed him myself.

Then the bullfrog got up and began walking up and down and croaked out a new speech against him. And once he got so excited he started swelling up the way he did sometimes, and we all had to sit on him to keep his stomach from bursting. After the frog the rabbit would stand up and say Old Joe was all right. But you know the rabbit never can remember what he's doing from one tail shake to the next. A couple of times right in the middle of a speech he ran off with a trashy brown rabbit that came up and whispered he'd found a barrel of carrots. And we had to stop the trial until we could go and bring him back.

And then finally all the speeches were finished and everybody got quiet. And I went off to the woods with some other raccoons and two turtles and a

muskrat that were the jury. And we sat
around eating some berries and talked,
and then we went back to the trial.
And Judge Black asked what we'd decided. And I said we found him guilty.

The fox acting Old Joe began crying. And Judge Black told him to stand
up and be sentenced. And the Judge
looked at him, kind of sad, and said,

"Honesty is the best policy," and then thought a little while and told him, "Might makes unright." And then he cleared his throat and said, "I sentence you to swallowing a jug for life."

And the fox in the alligator skin began acting like he was crazy, rolling on the ground and moaning and hollering, "Oh, not that." Because he knew what an awful thing swallowing the jug was.

And then the trial broke up and I went off with the frog and found an old dried goose skin and we polished up the feathers with beeswax. And then we brought a jug a fisherman had left on the bank that we'd picked up and put away. If you watch close in the woods you can see animals carrying off things like that—you never know when they'll come in handy. And towards sundown we put the jug inside the goose skin, and went out to a pond in the swamp where a lot of geese were always swimming and where we knew Old Joe used to come when he wanted a goose dinner. We put our stuffed goose close to shore and waited. Pretty soon Old Joe came along and the other geese flew away in a hurry. But of course our goose stayed. And you could see Old Joe smiling an alligator smile and his mouth start watering. And then his terrible jaws opened and he swallowed the goose in one gulp.

The minute he swallowed it, he knew what'd happened. Maybe his teeth touched the edges of the jug, I don't know. And he began roaring something awful, and trying to cough up what he'd swallowed. Because an alligator'd rather have anything done to him than have a jug in his stomach. It makes him so light he can't swim smooth, and he can't dive under birds and animals in the water. And worst of all he can't sink down to get in his hole, even to sleep for the winter.

All night we could hear him trying to cough up the jug, and all the next day and the day after. And even though we knew how bad he was, with all that coughing he looked really pitiful. He went around with the jug inside him all the rest of the summer. I guess he'd have starved to death if we hadn't fed him some melons and corn. And then cold weather came and he tried to crawl in his hole to get warm; and the air in the jug wouldn't let him go down. Alligators hate cold weather and we could see him laying out on the bank all night, shivering so hard the birds in the trees around him couldn't sleep because of the way his shivers shook the branches.

Finally Judge Black said he'd been punished enough, even though he had a life sentence. We found Old Joe and I took a long cat-tail and stood on one side of him and J. C. stood with a cat-tail on the other.

"Say *a-a-a-h*," we told him. And then when his jaws opened we put the cat-tails down his mouth and we tickled his throat together.

He gave a terrible cough that almost

knocked us over. And the jug popped out and dropped into the bayou. The Judge made Old Joe fish it out and carry it tied around his neck for another month just for a reminder. But I saw right away he could have left it in the bayou. Old Joe was a different alligator.

All the time he went around making speeches to his alligator friends, trying to get them to change their ways. He kept telling 'em over and over as Judge Black said, "Crime doesn't pay." And plenty of times he came back with big teeth marks on his face and deep bruises in his hide, because the other alligators didn't like what he was saying.

Well, that took care of Old Joe. But we knew we hadn't fixed anything really. After all it was the man hunter we needed to be afraid of; he'd be a hundred times as bad if he ever really got started.

But none of us still had any idea of the terrible thing that was going to happen. Not even the big old turtle out in the middle of the swamp who could tell floods and frost and all kinds of bad weather and trouble by the aches in his neck and his bones.

ℓℓ

II

WELL, everything was quiet for a while. We got a little worried one afternoon when that beaver you saw a while ago came around, and if you haven't seen many beavers their long teeth can give you a scare.

But when we looked close we could see there wasn't anything to be afraid of, he was so tired and miserable.

"I'm just looking for some animals to stay with," he said. "Just a place where I can sit around and talk. I'm so lonesome I could die." He chewed the apple I gave him like he hadn't eaten for a month and swallowed it, core and all.

"I guess you know the most important thing about beavers is chopping a tree right. If a beaver can't chop a tree straight so it falls where the other beavers want it, they throw you out of the beaver camp. I'm one of those beavers."

Well, spring had come again with some hot days and we'd been talking how nice it'd be to fix up a big pool in the swamp under the trees where we could go swimming and cool off. And you can't beat a beaver for building a

dam and making a pool. So I asked him if he thought he could fix a pool for us.

His face shone like he'd shined it with waxberries. "I'll cut down some trees right away," he said. "I'm feeling fine now and I'll make 'em land right where I aim 'em. Close as a beaver's whisker."

He picked out a cottonwood and sharpened his teeth on a little stone he carried. And then he cut the tree quick as those big saws the loggers bring and he aimed it to fall toward the bayou. But it fell just the other way on the bank and pretty near hit Judge Black and the rabbit.

The beaver ran up to see if they were hurt, and then he started crying. "It won't happen again," he sobbed. "If you give me another chance, I'll be sure to do it right next time."

J. C. the fox was terribly mad and said we ought to make him go away.

"He's a dangerous animal," J. C. said. "You can see by his face he's half-witted. It's because his teeth are so long, they're growing into his brain, the way it is sometimes with beavers. If we have a crazy fellow like that with those teeth around some morning we'll wake up and wonder why we feel so funny. It'll be because we'll all be murdered."

But Judge Black didn't agree. "Do as you would be done by," he said.

So we let the beaver stay.

Funny, you get one animal in trouble like that, and pretty soon you get another. I guess news spreads fast in the

swamp, what with the bees and butter-
flies and the ants going everywhere and
the blue jays having nothing to do but
talk. And maybe they cut marks in the
trees to show where the animals are
good-natured and'll give 'em something
to eat, like I've heard men tramps do in
the towns. Anyway it wasn't a week
after the beaver came that a big old
goose walked in with his feathers all

battered and his body all skinny. And he asked if he could live with us, too. He'd been thrown out of his flock, just like the beaver.

"I'm a watchman goose," he told us. "Geese always have a watchman that stays awake at night when the other geese are sleeping. That way they can tell when something's coming that'll hurt 'em, like alligators and wildcats and foxes. But someway I always fell asleep and one night twenty geese got killed when I didn't hear some foxes."

His eyes filled with tears. "That was the most awful morning I ever saw. The other geese all gathered around me. And they all beat their wings at me the way geese do. And they hissed me out of the flock forever."

39

His voice got all choky and he had to be quiet for a minute, he couldn't keep on talking. "But I'm all right now," he said. "I've been sitting up every night, practicing and practicing. And I never once close my eyes. All I ask is just to try me once. I'll be sure to stay awake."

Well, we always have somebody on watch for the hunter or any bad animals that might turn up, so we told him we'd try him out that night. We put him on guard and were all sleeping fine when I woke up dreaming the woods were on fire. And I jumped up and the search-light of the hunter was shining in my face, not twenty coon tails away. And the goose, supposed to be on guard, was standing with his head tucked under his wing, sleeping like a baby.

I shouted at the others and they waked up and ran off, and the hunter didn't get anybody. But things like that are bad for your nerves and they bother your stomach; the fruit and things I borrowed from the farm at the edge of the swamp didn't taste right for a week, maybe. The goose broke down and cried, like the old beaver.

"Something just came over me," he moaned. "But it'll never happen any more. If I ever go to sleep again I'll give myself to the fox for a Thanksgiving dinner."

And J. C. the fox looked at him and nodded his head fast. "I think we ought to let him live with us," he declared. "It's like Judge Black says. We ought to think of charity." Though I didn't like the way he spoke the words.

So we let the goose stay too.

After that all the time the goose and the beaver used to go around together, because misery likes company the way the Judge said.

Well, from then on it seemed like our quiet times were over. Next night the hunter came again and this time he brought a big bloodhound. Most people don't train bloodhounds for hunting; but when they do it's terrible. All night we saw him running through the

swamp, his eyes red-hot like stove lids in winter, his jaws all dripping with foam. And then he'd stop and put his paw near his mouth and give an awful howl. A bloodhound holds his paws that way to throw his voice so you can't tell which way he's coming. And if you're on the ground the noise locks your jaws and paws; and when you can't move he runs up to you. And of course after that you're done.

Morning came, and half a dozen of the swamp animals we knew were gone forever. The bloodhound came back that night and every night for a while after. And then one morning a couple of our best friends were missing; one a fox that J. C. said had been just like a father to him, and a raccoon that'd been an old treemate of mine and had taught me how to watch two bees flying and where they met was where you'd find their honey.

"Things can't go on this way," I said to the others. "We've got to stop the bloodhound, the way we did Old Joe. And maybe if we stop him we'll stop the hunter too."

"What'll we do?" asked the rabbit, who was serious for once. "When I hear him coming and he throws his voice, I get stiff as those iron animals they have in the front yards of those big houses at Vicksburg."

"We'll get some onions and put 'em in our paw-tracks," I answered. "They say a bloodhound can't stand the smell of onions. It'll keep them from tracking every time."

Next day we went early and picked a lot of wild onions that were growing along the bayou. And wherever we walked we rubbed the onions in our paw-marks. The bloodhound came after dark and put his nose to the ground; and he smelt the onions and started to sneeze like he was going to choke. I guess the onions would have stopped most other bloodhounds. But they just couldn't

stop this one. He kind of shook himself a couple of times, and drew in some deep breaths, and then came on sniffing and tracking. Next day we tried peppermint, and after that some pepper I found in the kitchen at the farm. But he just sneezed and coughed a little again; they weren't any better than the onions.

Things got worse and worse and

more and more of our friends kept on disappearing. And then one afternoon I had an idea. There was a hollow tree full of bees near our camp and I hurried over. I rolled myself in mud till just my eyes were showing so I wouldn't get stung, the way you always do when you're after honey. And then I muddied myself some more and climbed the tree to the hive. The queen bee was there, kind of fat and not looking very bright and wearing a kind of gold crown; and there were a lot of old bees standing around and a bald-headed old bee was by her.

The bald-headed bee stared at me a long time and I could see he was mighty suspicious. "Your face looks very familiar," he said. "Aren't you the raccoon stole a pound of honey out of this hive two weeks ago and another pound last Thursday?"

I shook my head and answered in a hurry. "That must have been my twin brother came up from Frogmore," I said. "He looks just like me and always gets me in trouble." And then I told the bald-headed bee just what I'd come for.

He talked it over with the queen and the other old bees and there was a lot of arguing and buzzing. Lucky for me, it turned out the bees were mad at the bloodhound and the hunter.

"They're ruining the swamp," buzzed the fat queen bee, straightening up her crown that was slipping a little. "They've knocked down all our best sunflowers and trampled our best sweet clover."

So I didn't have to do much talking to get them to do what I wanted.

I hurried back to our camp feeling pretty fine. What I'd asked the bees to do was simple. I'd heard from some raccoons about a new kind of fence that would give you a shock if you just touched the wire; they were using 'em on the big plantations to keep out animals and people. I figured we'd make a bee fence around our camp, to keep out the bloodhound and the hunter.

Next day you could see bees moving in from everywhere and the air sounded like a hundred sawmills going. The hunter had started coming in the afternoon now, and pretty soon we heard his gun shooting. And then we heard the bloodhound rushing through the bushes, sniffing so loud it was like the *Tennessee Belle* puffs when she's trying to make a landing along the river. And then all of a sudden the bloodhound gave a terrible yell.

"I'm on fire!" he hollered.

And we heard him racing away, and I knew the bee fence had him.

He jumped into the bayou till the stings cooled a little. And then he came again in a different place, and ran back,

howling louder. Half a dozen times he
tried to break through, and each time
he ran away yelping. But he was stub-
born and came back next morning and
once or twice a day for a month nearly.

He didn't look like a dog any more; his
head and body were so swollen up he
looked just like a pumpkin.

We didn't see him for a while, and
we thought maybe we were rid of him
and his hunter master. And then one
afternoon we saw him coming through

the palmetto again, sniffing louder and
louder the closer he came to where we
were staying. And I ran off to tell the
bees, because I knew that lately they
hadn't been watching.

There wasn't anybody there but the
bald-headed old bee, and he looked
awful worried. "They've all gone
away," he said. "I stayed because I've
got one of my usual swamp colds. The
queen and all of 'em are having a meeting in a field of wild asters that's just

started blooming. There's a bee from up North telling 'em how to get more honey to the flower and how to put less wax in the hives."

I went back to our camp and heard the bloodhound coming closer and closer. And then he was almost on top of us, and we all thought we were finished. But he rushed on past us as if we weren't there and then stopped—at a hollow tree full of honey.

He stood there, howling and digging at the bark, just like he'd treed a possum. The hunter came running and saw what the hound'd tracked and scolded him something awful. And the bloodhound sniffed the ground and ran off again and stopped this time by an old broken shed that I knew had the best hive in the swamp. Next day he came again; but it was always the same. All those bee stings had done something funny to his nose. He couldn't track anything but honey.

I saw him once after that going through the woods and pointing with his paw up, the way hunting dogs do. And I saw what he was pointing was a bee.

The hunter got rid of him right away, and the old horse that lives over on the farm told me he'd got himself a job working for the police down in New Orleans. But I don't think he'll last there very long.

Well, we had maybe a week's rest and then we heard shots again and we knew the hunter was back. And this time it looked like he was mad because of what happened to the bloodhound. He set out traps, too, and I watched where he put 'em. And I turned every one of 'em over with my paw so they wouldn't catch a thing. Coons have known how to do that ever since trapping started.

"Maybe he'll be arrested," I said. "He's hunting out of season. And every animal in the swamp knows he's an awful thief besides. Plenty of times I've seen him stealing sugar from the barges they tie up along the Mississippi. And then he takes it off in his boat and sells it in town. The steamboat people are awful mad and they've offered a big reward. Maybe the game wardens or the sheriff'll catch him."

And we kept hoping they would. But they didn't.

He kept getting worse and worse.

"I'll stop him," said the beaver. "I'll chop down a tree so it smashes his boat and then he can't come into the bayou at all."

He sharpened his teeth on the stone again and started sawing a big poplar. But when the hunter came instead of hitting the boat, the tree fell on the bank, and almost killed the fox and a couple of possums.

A few days later we heard the hunter again and this time he was looking for frogs. The Indian Bayou Glee Club had been doing fine, getting ready for the big concert of the year over at the animal picnic grounds near Mud Lick. That's where the animals have the big

get-together and athletic meet before a lot of 'em go in for the winter. They have contests for the best glee clubs, and rabbit and deer jumping, and raccoon and possum contests to see who can climb a tree fastest. And our old bullfrog had found a frog from Clay Hole could sing tenor better than any frog that had ever been heard in our part of the Valley. His voice was so wonderful when he started singing all the animals would stop whatever they were doing to come around him and listen.

And our old frog would start swelling up, he'd be so proud; we always kept moss soaking in cold water to have it ready to put on his head and his stomach. Everybody knew that with the Clay Hole frog helping, the Indian Bayou club would win the singing contest sure.

Well, when we heard the hunter's boat the Clay Hole frog was sitting beside the bayou. And he had three young frogs that belonged to the club, teaching 'em how to eat slippery elm bark and keep their voices smooth.

"You'd better start moving," I said. "That hunter's boat comes fast."

But you know how those singers are, they haven't got much sense. And then all of a sudden the boat shot out, and the searchlight swung down the bayou. And when it swung away again, the four frogs were all in the hunter's bag with fifty others like 'em.

Well, I don't have to tell you how it was. Our old bullfrog just stood there with his eyes popping like marbles.

He didn't say a word for a minute, just turned kind of white and then he turned red and then he turned kind of purple. "It's the crack of doom," he croaked. "Doom and disaster."

You couldn't blame him for feeling bad. He'd lost his finest voices. Besides the wonderful frog tenor, he'd lost his three best young ones, high *do*, low *mi*, and middle *fa*, and he'd just trained them perfect. And without those four we all knew there wasn't a chance of winning the contest.

But raccoons are smart and they can

act fast. I knew that hunters are crazy about foxes.

I turned to J. C. "Run up on the bank," I said. "And give some fox barks good and loud. Out where the hunter'll be sure to hear you."

Most times when I'd say something, J. C.'d start arguing. But this time he did what I told him. "O.K.," he answered, and gave some good barks, and let the searchlight swing across his tail for a second. And the hunter gave a yell and rushed after him into the bushes.

A minute later I was in the boat, cutting open the bag of frogs with my teeth and letting them all go free.

As soon as we were off in a safe place our bullfrog started the others singing "Adeline," to try out their voices. The frog tenor from Clay Hole was all right; but the three young ones were so out of tune every note hurt your ears.

Our old frog listened and wiped his eyes. "The young ones are done forever," he croaked. "They've all been scared flat."

Well, I guess the hunter didn't like losing those frogs, and after that night he got meaner and meaner. Sometimes he wouldn't come down the bayou now, but'd try to catch us when we weren't ready. I'd see him walking across the farm, past the big herd of cows that was always at the edge of the swamp, where they could nibble the swamp grass and bushes. And each time he brought big guns that roared like cannon and would kill you sure, even if you were half a mile away. And so many of my best friends were missing, it looked like there wasn't going to be a single animal left in the swamp.

And then the way we always did when there was trouble—we had a meeting. And they all asked me to figure out something.

"I'll try," I said. "But this hunter's so mean he knows all the tricks. It isn't going to be easy."

Like I told you this fellow was a big thief, stealing sugar all the time from the river barges. Well, one morning after

our meeting, the sheriff was driving along in his car when he saw some sugar spilled, right across the highway. And he followed where it led, and it led straight to the hunter's cabin. 'Course the sheriff arrested him then, and they sent him off to the penitentiary. And I hear they found out about a lot of other bad things and he's going to stay there for life. The sheriff collected the reward and put up a new chicken house. And I'm not saying I don't want him to have the money. But just the same, if you'd have looked close that morning, all along that trail of sugar you'd have seen the marks of raccoon paws.

III

THINGS were quiet after that and for a year we had a wonderful time. And then one day the terrible thing happened, worse than any of us had ever thought of, even in our worst dreams.

We were sitting around, eating and talking and watching some muskrats thickening up their fur with pokeberry oil because they said it was going to be a cold winter.

The whistle of the *Tennessee Belle* sounded across the trees from the river, on her way down to New Orleans.

I stopped eating the persimmon I had in my paws to listen.

"Now the hunter's in jail, I've been thinking more and more how lucky we are to be living at Catfish," I said. "In summer there's always the river and the bayou to keep you cool. And in winter there are wonderful warm holes to go down in if you want to. And you don't even have to think about your meals, there's always so much to eat. And for music you can always hear those steamboat whistles blowing."

"I've written a poem about Catfish Bend," giggled the rabbit, though I couldn't see anything to giggle about. "It goes this way:

> Armadillos like Texas,
> Polar bears like Alaska.
> But if I'll ask you——"

We didn't let him go any further.

You had to be very firm with a rabbit.

He was hurt for a minute. "Well, anyway," he said. "I was talking to that white rabbit just came in yesterday from up river. He said he was sorry for the other animals that'd never been here. Because he said the Bend was the place he'd always been looking for. It was animal heaven."

Judge Black took a little of the milk and sunflower seeds that he was trying for a new cereal, because being a vegetarian he was always wanting to figure out new ways of making his vegetables nice. "East, West, Catfish Bend is the best," he said. "There's no place like home."

The rabbit had just asked the Judge if he could finish what was left of the cereal, when the fox came running up, breathing so hard it looked like the fur on his chest would fly off.

"I've just been over to the Catfish store," he panted. "I was down in the cellar getting some corn. And I could hear the farmers talking through the floor. The State's just rented all the swamp to a hunting club that's got all the biggest hunters in the country. They're coming in early tomorrow, hundreds and hundreds of 'em, from Vicksburg and Memphis and St. Louis and everywhere. We've got to get out or we'll all be killed. It's worse than a Mississippi flood."

None of us made a sound. It got so quiet under the trees you could hear the caterpillars that weren't born yet turning in their cocoons. And near you there was just the sound of the fox breathing, low and mournful now, like the wind before a storm.

I thought I'd seen some bad times, the night the levee broke and we were almost drowned, and the day the woods caught fire and we were almost burned to death. But this was worse than anything; so bad we couldn't believe it. We

all went over to the store and listened. And then we knew there wasn't any doubt; what the fox had said was true. We were going to lose our home, the place where we had lived and our fathers and grandfathers had lived, farther back than even the old turtle could remember; and he knew the time when you had to watch out for buffaloes that might step on you. The worst thing that could happen to anybody had happened to us; we had to leave Catfish Bend.

We got back to our camp in the swamp again. And we just stood there, too shocked to move. And then we remembered the hunters would be coming early, so we had to get out fast.

We started to pack up. But the frog wouldn't begin.

"It's no use doing anything," he croaked. "It's the crack of doom."

But we talked to him a minute and then he joined the others getting ready.

I tell you it's heart-breaking to give up a place where you've spent all your life; the trees you've had holes in and filled up with the knick-knacks a coon likes to collect, mirrors and silver coins and pieces of milk bottles. We didn't have time to pack any of our things right. We had to leave half of them behind. And half of what we took got broken.

At frog second-breakfast time, that's just before dawn, we started to go away. And as the sun rose we could see the hunters coming, some by themselves, and some in twos and threes, and some in fives and tens; big men and little men, and fat men and skinny men, some of them wearing fancy clothes with colored caps and stripes that made them look like silly parrots, and some of them with heavy coats and boots for walking in the swamp. But all of them had guns and all of them had that terrible hunter look in their eyes, the look a hungry weasel gets in a chicken coop full of hens.

And at a safe distance ahead where the hunters couldn't see them, there were long lines of animals, deer and woodchucks and possums and rabbits, mothers and fathers and sleepy children, all going away, like us, they didn't know where. It had turned bitter cold in the night, too, and there was ice on the ground, and some of the mothers and children were crying. And you could see the tears freezing on their fur.

Well, pretty soon we came to the highway that ran along the river. And we started walking at the side so as not to be hit by the big auto trucks bumping past us every minute. They were terrible, all those trucks, the horns that made your ears feel like somebody was sticking thorns in 'em, and the awful smells that made you cough. And then to make it worse, some boys came and began shooting at us with air rifles. So we moved over to the railroad and began walking the tracks.

"The trains are worse than the trucks," I said. "But there aren't nearly so many. And there aren't any boys with air rifles."

Going along those railroad ties was hard on all of us. Little stones were always squeezing in between your toes and you'd have to stop and pull them out, and splinters were always stabbing the soft places of your paws. But it was hardest on Judge Black. You know most snakes can't go fast very long, not having any legs. You could see how tired he was getting every time we came to a hole between the ties and he had to wind himself across.

"You ought to stop for a while," I told him. "The rest of us can wait."

But he shook his head and went right on. "I'm doing fine," he said.

It got colder and colder all day, and when dark came we found a big empty barrel. And we crawled inside and tried to cover ourselves with a few leaves and some bits of straw. But it snowed in the night, and we woke up all white. And my nose was so cold I couldn't feel it was there, and my whiskers were all turned to ice.

We started up the tracks again, and a bitter wind was blowing. Pretty soon a train came along behind us, and the wind was howling so loud we didn't hear a sound. And all of a sudden it was right on top of us and we had to jump for our lives. We landed in a little creek just frozen over. And we crawled out covered with ice and mud and we all wished we were dead.

The frog halted on a broken tie. His head and feet looked like glass, and icy steam was coming up from his back. "I'm not going on any more," he croaked. "They say when you die by cold you never know. I'm going to stop right here on the tracks and let the cold freeze me till I'm dead."

And a lot of the other animals said the same thing. But Judge Black and I made them go on.

We traveled this way day after day.

And when I stop to think what we went through, I don't know what kept us alive. Because with the cold weather there wasn't any food, and half the time we were starving. Once in a while we were lucky and we'd find a freight car, full of bags of corn meal or oranges. And we'd eat till the brakeman came with a stick, looking for tramps. And I'd call "Low bridge!" and we'd all jump out the car door.

And one time we were so hungry we could hardly stand and we found a car full of bananas. And there were some terrible-looking spiders big as muskmelons out in front and I thought at first they were sentries. So I asked them and they bowed awful polite and answered in some funny kind of language, and I couldn't understand one word.

But the fox came in from another car and he'd been down in Texas, near Mexico. "They're Spaniards from South America," he said. "They call themselves tarantulas."

And he asked them in Spanish if they were watching the bananas. And they bowed again—everybody bows that way in South America—and they said goodness no, they weren't watching anything; they just came with the bananas on a boat for the ride.

"They say to eat as many as we like," J. C. told us. "Just so we throw the skins out the door, because they make the floor so slippery. They've got some old tarantulas along, and with tarantulas having so many feet to slip on they don't want 'em to trip and fall."

That was the only good day we had in weeks, I guess. All the rest of the time we'd just drag ourselves on, asking every animal we met if they knew a place that'd do for our home.

And then another terrible disaster came. We were walking along the tracks one day and we saw a little town ahead. And we decided we'd travel around it because towns for us generally meant trouble. We were going through a gully when two boys came with air rifles, and they started shooting. And before we could run off they'd taken aim and shot Judge Black in the back. We saw right away he was hurt terribly, and we didn't know what to do. All the other snakes were in for the winter and there wasn't an animal anywhere to ask what kind of medicine to give him. We found a big sewer pipe near a bridge close by and carried the Judge inside. And we all stood close around and breathed up and down his back to try to keep him warm. All night we stayed up with him and he lay so still we thought he'd die before morning.

And then I heard a cow moo in a barn a little way off and I went over and asked her for a little milk, because I knew Judge Black liked milk better than anything. And she gave it to me and I brought it back in an old milk bottle I found and rubbed some of it on the Judge's lips.

And then his eyes opened a little and

he raised up and looked at us. "True friends are half the battle," he said, and lay down again. And we knew he was going to live.

We stayed in the sewer a couple of days until we thought we could move him. Things had been bad before, but they were terrible now with Judge hurt, especially with a hurt back. Sometimes we'd tie him to a long stick and the fox and I would sling the stick between us. Or if his wound was hurting too much we'd make a kind of litter of branches and four of us would carry it on our shoulders. Though I hated to do it because the frog couldn't really walk with anybody—he always wanted to hop.

Plenty of times Judge Black would

lean over to me on the litter when he thought the others weren't listening. "It isn't fair to burden you this way," he said. "You go on and leave me to the buzzards."

'Course I'd pay no attention, maybe just put some moss and leaves under his back and make him ride a little easier.

Well, they say that when one bad thing happens more trouble comes right away. We'd been going north all the time and we were walking the tracks near Helena in Arkansas. And we began to hear stories about two outlaw rats in the country around, murdering and robbing every animal they met. I told all our animals to stay close together, because the outlaws wouldn't be likely to bother so many. Everybody did what I said. That is everybody except the rabbit. Just when we were passing a hill where we'd heard the rats were living in a cave, he stopped all of a sudden and sniffed.

"I smell a lettuce field," he said in his squeaky voice.

"You're crazy," I told him. "It's the dead of winter. There's no lettuce growing anywhere."

"Oh catnip!" he answered. "Do you

think I don't know lettuce when I smell it?"

And before we could stop him he was away off, running in those wild rabbit jumps of his straight toward the outlaws' hill. And in a couple of minutes we heard a loud squeal and we knew the outlaws had him.

We formed a rescue party as soon as we could and spread over the hill trying to find him. It took time, and I was all by myself after dark when I came on the cave where the outlaws were staying. I crawled to the entrance, and hiding in the shadows, looked inside to see what was happening. They had the rabbit there, all right. I could see him locked up in a big rat trap that I guess somebody had set out for the outlaws;

now instead they were using it as a kind of cage to keep the animals they captured. They were sitting around the rabbit, chewing licorice root, and spitting and looking mean, and talking.

"I hear there's a couple of rich mink coming down next week," said the first outlaw, a skinny, terrible-looking rat, with a big hollow place in his forehead

from a hatchet and one of his wicked eyes missing. "You catch one of them mink and you can hole in and not have to work for a year maybe."

"Them minks'll fight you too much," said the second outlaw, a kind of chunky rat with his ears mashed flat against his head and a tooth right in front that was broken. "I like to rob animals that's easy, like rabbits and squirrels. There's a squirrel coming through in the morning, they says, that's carrying everything he's saved up in all his holes ever since he was born. I'm sure going to lay for that squirrel."

They turned to the rabbit now and started talking how they'd divide him for supper. They made him walk up and down around the cage maybe ten times so they could look him all over. And then I crawled out to the hill again and ran back to tell the news to the others.

We hadn't said a word about the rabbit to Judge Black. He'd been sick worse than ever the last few days. We had to carry him on the litter all the time, his back was hurting so terribly.

But he heard us talking and spoke up from the litter. "We've got to save the rabbit," he said. "And it's my duty to do it. Rats are afraid of a blacksnake more than anything."

And he told us how before he became a vegetarian, like so many other blacksnakes he'd been an official rat catcher, working in the fish store on the Vicksburg wharf.

We told him that he was too sick; when those rats, big as bulldogs, saw how weak he was they'd tear him to pieces.

He closed his eyes a minute because talking tired him so, and then opened them and raised his head. "Better a hero in a grave than a coward on a throne," he said.

There wasn't anything to do but the way he wanted. We picked up the litter and carried him to the cave, and put him down at the entrance. And he crawled off the litter somehow and moved inside. And then he opened up his jaws and hissed, like the most terrible blacksnake in the Valley. And those outlaw rats took one look—and they knocked each other over they ran so fast, trying to get into a weasel hole that was the cave's back door.

When they were gone I let the rabbit out of the trap and scolded him for causing us so much trouble. And I hurried over to Judge Black lying by the entrance. And then I saw that like I thought, it'd all been too much for him. He was stretched out on his back, breathing hard, and his whole body was shivering. And when a snake shivers it's the worst shivering anywhere, being so long and skinny. It took him a couple of hours before he could stop. And then I brought the rabbit to thank him and say he was sorry.

But the Judge smiled at him the way sick people smile and said he didn't need an apology. "A good deed is its own reward," he said. And he turned his head away so we couldn't see how he was hurting.

All winter we kept wandering. And then one day I went down to a city dump we were passing to see if I could find a few scraps of bread maybe. An old cat was standing around and we got to talking.

"There's a big island out in the Mississippi near Memphis," he said. "Way I've heard it's the cat's pajamas. Plenty to eat and no people or hunters. But it's no good for me or most other cats because cats generally like a town . . . Excuse me, I see some funeral pieces thrown away and that's what I came for. A friend of mine was hurt a little in a cat-fight yesterday. And I want to bring him some flowers."

That island was the first place we'd heard of in months that sounded like it might do. It took us a long time to get there with Judge Black being so sick, but we saw the island at last. It had white sandy beaches all along the water and in the middle were big cotton-woods and pines. We didn't know how we'd get out to it because there weren't any boats and it was too far to swim. And then the beaver said he'd cut down some trees and let them fall in the river so we could float over on the trunks. He chopped down some big poplars, but of course they fell wrong, and they were too heavy for us to move to the water. Lucky, though, I found some logs tied up at the bank and we climbed on and steered 'em over.

The island was fine when we first got there. The day was lovely and warm and we sat on the beach and swam and bathed and put Judge Black on his litter out in the sun. And J. C. the fox, did some of his tricks and cracked some jokes, and I laughed for the first time in so long it hurt my stomach. The

animals that lived there, the deer, and the otters, and the woodchucks and the squirrels, were all nice and friendly, too, and we thought our troubles were over. But toward twilight I noticed they were all getting nervous. And when I asked why they said they were worried. Every night just after dark a big panther always ran out from the trees in the middle of the island. He'd come there from the hills back of Hot Springs, Arkansas, and before that from the Great Divide in Colorado. They said his name was Perceval, which I thought was a pretty funny name for a panther.

Well, it got dark, and pretty soon we heard a terrible roar like thunder. And all the animals shouted "It's Perceval!"

and ran off down the beaches. And then the roaring was closer and the panther came crashing through the bushes. And we could see his long teeth shining in the moonlight, like ghost teeth tipped with fire. He rushed all around the island trying to catch things. And some of the rabbits and the little animals would call out "Please, Perceval," and he'd only holler louder. It kept everybody awake all night, and after a couple of weeks I was getting worn out. And I called the animals together.

"I've been watching this panther close," I said. "And he's really not a bad animal. It's just his name Perceval that makes him want to act so tough. Let's call him a tough name and I bet it'll make him act nice."

He came that night and all of us that could climb trees were way up in the branches.

"Scarface!" I shouted at him when he roared under me after a rabbit. And all through the trees other voices came calling "Scarface!" And I wish you could have seen him when we all said it together.

The first time he stopped and looked like he wasn't hearing right, and then he looked madder for a minute. The second time he looked like you do when you've lost your way in the woods, kind of worried and wondering. And then the third time he smiled. And I knew our worries about panthers were over.

In a couple of days he wasn't bothering anybody and in a couple of weeks he was everybody's friend, sitting around with us under the stars, and telling us stories of the cowboys and the big Rocky Mountain sheep along the Great Divide.

After that everything would have been all right. But a gas boat full of hunters came over from Memphis one day, and pretty soon hunters came all the time. So we had to move on again. Well, we kept going up the Mississippi toward St. Louis—some of the animals had heard there was some fine country around there on the Missouri—and things got worse and worse. We passed a lot of farms and cotton plantations and big cattle ranches people were start- ing along the river, like they had out West, and we saw other islands they were turning into cattle ranches, too. But we never found anywhere we could stay. We went to some places that had pretty woods with lots of holes in 'em that'd make wonderful homes for an animal. But when we looked close we could see every hole was packed tight with raccoons and rabbits and foxes, just like ants in an anthill. The govern- ment was building some big dams back in the hills and had flooded the land all around. So the animals had to leave by the thousands and take the nearest places they could find. There wasn't an empty hole in a hundred miles.

Winter was coming on again, a bad winter, too; the cold wind froze you so hard you'd have to look down at your feet to see if they were moving.

Someway we had got through one winter, I don't know how. But I knew we could never get through another. And St. Louis and the Missouri were still a long way off. Judge Black had left his litter now, but you could see from his eyes he wouldn't last very long if we didn't get somewhere he could rest. And it was the same with others. We were all so thin even the buzzards that had been flying over our heads stopped following us and flew off somewhere else. When we died we wouldn't be worth the trouble of eating.

I called everybody together one day after a couple of our old animals had stopped and said they couldn't travel any farther. It was under a big rocky cliff by the river.

I waited a minute for quiet and then I started talking. "I'm not going on this way any more," I said. "I'm not going to wander the rest of my life like a thief and an outcast. There's only one thing to do. Catfish Bend's our home, the place that belongs to us and that we belong to. I want us all to go back to Catfish and fight it out with the hunters."

Well, everybody started talking at once, and some said this and some the other. Of course you have to decide things like that by a vote. And when I asked the animals that thought the way I did to raise their paws, every paw went up like it was one.

But I didn't want any mistakes. So

I warned them of the dangers. "If anybody wants to quit, now's the time," I said. "Everybody'll turn their backs and those that want to can walk off and nobody'll even see 'em go."

We all turned our backs—and when we turned around again I saw not an animal was missing.

The Indian Bayou Glee Club came up and we all sang "Star Spangled Banner." And then we formed a line under the cliff, and the Club sang "Tenting Tonight" and marching songs, like a band, and we started down toward Catfish.

IV

We traveled along the bank and then we rode on some sawmill logs floating down the Mississippi. We climbed off when we came to Catfish Bend and hurried across the levee. And we saw the swamp, and I closed my eyes, it made me feel so sad. The hunters had trampled down all the wild flower beds and the wild corn and the soft pussy willows; big black patches showed where they'd burned the grass and cane so they could catch the animals easier. All the branches were shot off the trees where they'd been aiming at the squirrels and possums; the old tree where I'd lived for so long had fallen and was laying all black on the ground. They'd burned it trying to smoke me out because they thought I was inside.

The hunting season was just opened, and we went a little way farther in the swamp, and then we saw the hunters all over. Some were in tents and some in kind of houses made of their automobiles and some were just carrying blankets. Most of the animals had gone away when we did; there must have been a hundred hunters to every deer and coon and possum.

I saw the old turtle, who had stayed because hunters don't generally bother turtles, and I asked him what was happening.

He rubbed his beak against a log to

polish a scarred place on the side. "I've lived here since the Indian time," he said, "and I never saw anything like it. You see what those hunters have done to the Bend. They've killed or driven off everybody and ruined everything. Now day after tomorrow they're having a big shoot, with prizes for duck-calling and target-shooting and the most animals they can catch. And some of the big State people are coming, too, to find out how the hunters are doing. They want to see if they ought to keep on renting the swamp to the hunting club or take it back to be like it was before the hunters came."

We went on without making a sound, because we knew if we moved a leaf those hunters would start shooting. And we saw a place all surrounded by big canebrakes that looked pretty safe; and we stopped to unpack our belongings. We found a few holes in the ground and in the trees, and then we dug a few more for good measure. Because in a time like this you needed to have plenty of holes ready. And every once in a while we'd hear a shot in the distance, and we knew there'd be a new animal funeral in the morning.

I sat down by a tree stump and began to think. It was getting dark when I sat down and I stayed there all night thinking. And the others couldn't sleep and they sat up, too, keeping guard and listening. And all around we could hear the hunters crashing through the cane, trying to find us and kill us. Once in a while a shot'd whistle near us and we'd all jump down into a hole.

And then the sun came up and the hunters went away for a little while and the animals began to wash for breakfast. But I didn't move from my tree stump.

"I'm trying to figure out something," I said when the others asked me what I was doing. "This shooting meet to-morrow's the biggest thing for hunters anywhere. If we can spoil it someway, maybe they'll be discouraged and the State'll take the land back."

I'd just cleaned up a little when a bullet hit a branch right over our heads and another and another. And we ducked down into the holes again, and when we came out we had to wash all over. You can get an old hole nice and smooth, but in a new hole the dirt's al-ways falling.

The others sat down to have their breakfast, and I sat, too, but didn't take anything. "I'm not going to eat," I said. "I always think better on an empty stomach."

Then the rabbit turned around so suddenly he almost knocked over Judge Black's cereal. "Carrots! I've got it!" he said, with his mouth stuffed so full you could hardly understand him. "Just scatter their campfires the way we do garbage when we don't like people, and set all the woods on fire. That'll fix 'em fast."

I shook my head. "It'll fix us, too," I answered. "The panther told me about some Rocky Mountain sheep that tried it when he was traveling out West. That's what started those big forest fires you heard about and killed thousands of animals. And the sheep forgot they were burning up their own homes. They can't go back for twenty years."

The fox nibbled at some grapes he'd

found on the farm, and then his red face lighted. "How about sneaking up on 'em at night and turning their guns toward 'em and then just stepping on the triggers? That way they'd never come back unless somebody brought 'em in a box."

I thought that was pretty shocking, even for the fox. "We're not murderers, even if they are," I said. "And even if we wanted to, we couldn't do it. They sleep with their rifles right by their heads. They'd catch us before you could say gunpowder."

Judge Black looked worried. "Lawmakers cannot be lawbreakers," he said.

Sometimes when I can't get an idea it helps me if I go around and talk. And the hunters seemed to be off somewhere so I thought maybe it wouldn't be too risky.

I was walking through the swamp when all of a sudden I heard a sound that made me jump like a rabbit. A terrible shooting began up in the trees, fifty shots maybe, one after another. I thought for a minute the hunters had brought one of those awful machine guns I'd heard about the soldiers used in the war. And then I saw it was just a woodpecker, hammering away at a dead bough. "I haven't got any ideas," he said. "All this hammering isn't so good for your head. If you want somebody really smart go see that eagle named Old Gabe lives over in the big pine in the middle of the swamp. He's the boss of all the birds. He's the eagle on the silver dollar."

I climbed up to the top of the big pine where Old Gabe lived, so high I almost got dizzy. And I saw him, a big bald eagle, with his wings folded all stiff and solemn, because being an eagle's not the same as being a mouse.

"I used to catch raccoons like you," he said. "But of course I can't do it now they've put me on the silver dollar."

But he didn't have any ideas, either.

Well, I kept talking to everybody I met, dodging down a hole or racing up a tree whenever I saw a hunter. And still I couldn't think of anything. It was getting late, too, and the big shoot was tomorrow. If I didn't think of a plan fast there'd be no use thinking any more.

And then I saw some geese, honking in the sky, making the awful racket they always do, and I had my first idea. It was only a small idea. And I knew we still needed a big one or it wouldn't be any good to even try.

Well, it was twilight, and I was walking along the farm beyond the swamp when I saw the herd of cows standing at the edge of the trees where they always stood, nibbling the swamp grass and bushes. And then I remembered something I saw when we were wandering up the river. And I knew I had my big plan.

I looked to see there weren't any hunters around and went over to the head cow, fat and lazy from just eating and being milked, and mighty stuck up besides. I asked her if the cows would help us fight the hunters.

She pulled up some old leaves and gave her head a fancy toss, and some of the leaves fell on me. "I've always heard cows say crazy as a raccoon," she said.

"And now I know what they were meaning. We certainly won't help you fight the hunters. Some of the hunters are friends of the farmer we work for, and one of them's a rich fellow visits here every Sunday that the farmer hopes is going to marry his daughter. Winter's coming on when you can't eat or stay outside. Do you think we're going to take a chance on not staying in a nice warm barn, or not getting our hay? We'd do better to help the hunters fight you."

I tried to persuade her to change her mind, but all she did was to chew her cud, and cough it up at me in an insulting way, and after a while she wouldn't even answer. So I knew whatever we did, we'd have to do ourselves.

Well, I hurried back to our camp and told the others my plan. And we went off to the place where the shoot was to be and started to work right away. The hunters were all around us and we had to step past them soft as a field mouse's fur. And every once in a while there'd be a new shot. And we'd jump down in a hole and come up again and count ourselves to see if we all were still there.

It was long after dark when we finished and we all got ready for a nap. We couldn't go back to the place we had before; we needed to stay close by for what we had to do tomorrow. It was nicer than our other camp, but a thousand times more dangerous; here we were in the trees, right among the hunters. We could hear them talking how they'd catch us next day; their campfires were so close we could almost taste their cooking.

I turned to the watchman goose. "We're putting you on guard tonight," I said. "We've got a terrible day ahead and we all have to get some rest. This time our lives are in your hands. This time you've got to stay awake. Or it'll be the end of us all."

He became so excited you could see his gooseneck twisting into all kinds of funny shapes, like figure eight's and S's.

"I won't fail you," he said when he was calm again. "I swear to you I won't go to sleep. I'll die at my post before I do."

He took his place by a thicket of palmetto, and I saw him start marching back and forth over the ground, with his webbed feet coming down like a drum. And off in the distance you'd hear a bullet go *ping!* And he'd stretch his head and neck out stiff as a rifle, trying to hear, and then he'd start marching again.

I couldn't close my eyes because of all those bullets and hunters around, and my ears stuck straight up listening. But some young fellows with guns sneaked up like ghosts and even I didn't hear 'em.

But the goose heard and beat his wings. "Hunters!" he shouted. And he started a honking that would have made a possum, asleep for the winter, jump right out of his fur.

Three more times they came and

three more times he waked us. 'Course we congratulated him and told him what a fine goose he was, and what a wonderful watchman. He was so happy all night he kept talking and honking to himself, so loud I had to make him be quiet. I was afraid he'd bring the hunters again.

Well, morning came at last and the big shoot started. And I looked around to make sure no hunter was watching and climbed to the top of the highest tree where I could see everything that happened.

All the big State people were down below me, fat men in fancy suits and shirts with big diamond tie pins, and the big game wardens, tall skinny fellows, with shiny boots and wide hats like cowboys. They were all sitting in rows of camp chairs, laughing and smoking big cigars. And standing near 'em were the hunters, with the ten champions out in front, holding their guns like soldiers. Besides these were a couple of hundred people a little way off, that were just there looking on.

I'd been in the tree a little while when Judge Black came up and joined me.

I tried to get him to go down right away. "I don't think you ought to climb so high," I said. "It's bad for you with your back still hurting. And there'll probably be some bullets flying."

He shook his head. "I thought you might need me," he answered.

Then he looked down at the hunters and sighed. "I don't know why there are such people. I guess it takes all sorts to make a world."

Pretty soon a fat man in a red cap stood up before the State people and the hunters. And he made a little speech and said they'd start the duck-calling. And a fellow that looked like a midget began screwing up his face and making all those silly noises people think can fool a duck, though they wouldn't fool a duck made of wood. Well, he'd just been going half a minute maybe when I waved my tail as a signal. And all at once, everywhere from the trees there came the honking of a thousand geese, so loud it was like a road full of auto trucks, all blowing their horns together. You couldn't have heard that man duck-calling anymore than you could have heard the rabbit chewing a carrot. And a lot of people laughed, and that made the caller mad, and he tried to call louder. I guess he gave the calls a dozen times, and each time the geese honked him quiet. And then the other callers came and tried, and then they gave it up altogether.

And I signalled with my tail to the watchman goose that was sitting in another tree. And he motioned to the other geese to stop, and they flew away.

There was a scraping noise below me now and I looked down and saw the bullfrog coming up the tree. It's hard for a frog to climb a trunk and he never could have done it by himself. But a lot of little tree frogs were all around him, pushing and pulling, and squeezing and nudging, and boosting him up inch by inch.

He climbed out on the branch beside us and looked down at the hunters. "It's the day of judgment for 'em," he croaked.

There was a lot of target-shooting now, with all kinds of fancy guns and rifles. And then the man with the red cap made another speech, and said the hunters had ten minutes to get ready. And the ten champions took their guns and formed a line where the State people were sitting. And the other hunters bit off chews of tobacco and took their places behind 'em.

"This is the big shoot," I said to Judge Black. "All the rest was just for practice. This is what they call a game-bag hunt. When the man with the red cap fires his pistol, the hunters'll all start for the woods. And the fellow that has the most animals in his bag by sun-up tomorrow'll be the new hunter champion."

I saw the man with the red cap look at his watch. And I waved my tail again in signal. And at the top of every tree raccoon tails began to wave, all the way across the swamp to the farm where the herd of cows was feeding. I saw the last tail swing in a circle and then all the tails went down. And a minute later there was a terrible crash, and a big tree fell right by the stuck-up cow that said no when I asked her to help us. And she and the other cows and a bull that was there mooed and bellowed and began running; just like the times we'd seen lightning or something start 'em going on the ranches we passed up the river.

And then J. C. the fox, and some other foxes and raccoons, jumped out of the bushes.

"Stampede!" yelled J. C.

And he and the others began racing behind the cows, giving terrible whoops and coyote yells, and made 'em all run faster. J. C. drove 'em straight to the shooting ground. If the cows started turning the wrong way, J. C. and the others bit at their legs and barked and hollered louder.

Well, the man in the red cap was raising his pistol to fire when he saw those cattle come roaring. And all the other people saw 'em too; and they scattered like hens in a tornado. They dived into the woods, and plenty of the hunters threw away their guns, so they could run faster. And then the trees began crashing and tumbling down everywhere around 'em. The beaver had cut a lot of the trunks almost through so it took just a little push to make 'em fall. And he and the rabbit went around pushing 'em over. And this time every one of 'em fell right.

And Judge Black and the frog and I scrambled down from the trees and we joined J. C. driving the cattle. We pushed the people farther and farther back, over where the swamp was the thickest. And some of the hunters began shooting at each other, and I guess they went kind of crazy.

And then I talked to J. C., so hot

from running you could almost smell his fur burning. "Let the little fellows and the State people go," I said. "Chase the hunter champions. The State people are all right. We just had to remind 'em. But the hunters have been tormenting us for years. Now we'll show 'em what it's like to be hunted."

Well, night came and we got the hunters all separated in the woods. And then a few of us each took a different man and started him on a chase through the swamp, the way the hunters had done us so often. We drove a lot of moccasins and rattlesnakes toward 'em, and the men ran from the snakes and fell into sinkholes. They went down in the mud to their armpits and their chins; there wasn't a hunter left that when he

got out still had his rifle and ammuni-
tion.

"Get their guns and break 'em on
rocks and then throw 'em in the
bayou!" I shouted.

And you could hear guns splashing
everywhere, like otters jumping in summer.

We drove those hunters with the
snakes into awful pools and bogs where
the leeches and the mosquitoes ate 'em.
We drove 'em through briar patches
and thistle and thorn thickets till their
bodies were all scratched and their
clothes torn to pieces. And then when
we couldn't find any more snakes to
scare 'em, Judge Black'd rush in and out
of their legs, shaking some stones he'd
tied to his tail so they'd think he was a

rattler like the others. And when the hunters were so tired they couldn't run any farther, we went and waked Old Joe, the alligator, who was already sleeping for the winter. And he went after the hunters, too, giving terrible alligator hisses and roars, that they say'll break a farm window. And every once in a while, if things got quiet, the beaver would bring a tree crashing down; and the hunters'd start running again, and they'd fall in a new sinkhole.

The sun came up and we saw 'em in daylight. And you could hardly tell they were men. They looked more like some funny kind of caterpillars that lived all the time in the mud. You could hardly see they had arms or legs and you couldn't tell their ears or chins from their noses. They were so worn out, with every step you could hear their bones creak like the wheels of an old cotton wagon. They were so funny looking we shouldn't have done it but we couldn't help laughing like jaybirds. Instead of us being in their game bags, we could have caught them instead, if we'd only had a bag that was big enough.

Judge Black looked at the sun shining brighter every minute. "It's the way I've always said," he told us. "In every cloud there's a silver lining."

And the Indian Bayou Club sang "Dixie." And then we felt sorry for the hunters and we let them find their way home.

Well, even a man can get something

through his head, especially after a night like that. Those hunters had a pretty fair idea of what happened in the swamp. And when they came out every one of 'em said he was through with hunting for good. And just this morning we heard the wonderful news; the State people have taken Catfish away from the Hunting Club and made it what they call a game refuge with no hunters allowed at all. So Catfish Bend'll be better than ever. The State people acted mighty fast. I guess they didn't want us coming down where they live and starting any trouble in town.

The raccoon ended his story and took the comb from under the log and began smoothing his muddy fur again.

"It all happened last week," he said. "And we're working night and day getting the swamp straightened out. Haven't had a minute till now to clean up." He struggled with some thistles stuck in his fur. "Sometimes I wish I was smooth-skinned like a lizard. Raccoon hair tangles so easy."

I was just starting to answer when the big pine under which we were sitting crashed to the ground, passing so close my face wasn't the thickness of a coon whisker away.

I sat there as if I was frozen, too shocked to move.

And a minute later the old beaver came running.

He measured the distance from me

to where the tree fell, and smiled a smile full of pride. Then he turned to me in apology. "Sorry I scared you," he said. "But I have to keep my teeth in. Just in case one of those hunters comes back."

And after the battle all the animals who were part of the Pact awarded a silver star to the valorous seven for bravery beyond the call of duty.

—FROM THE DIARY OF JUDGE BLACK